When I First Met You,
Blue Kangaroo!

Emma Chichester Clark

HarperCollins *Children's Books*

*In memory of Margot Martini, the
little girl who sparked a movement.*

Collect all the fantastic books about Blue Kangaroo!

Where Are You, Blue Kangaroo?

It Was You, Blue Kangaroo!

What Shall We Do, Blue Kangaroo?

I'll Show You, Blue Kangaroo!

Merry Christmas, Blue Kangaroo!

Happy Birthday, Blue Kangaroo!

Come to School Too, Blue Kangaroo!

First published in hardback in Great Britain by HarperCollins Children's Books in 2015
First published in paperback in 2016

1 3 5 7 9 10 8 6 4 2

ISBN: 978-0-00-742511-2

HarperCollins Children's Books is a division of HarperCollins Publishers Ltd.

Text and illustrations copyright © Emma Chichester Clark 2015

Visit our website at: www.harpercollins.co.uk

Printed in China

Blue Kangaroo belonged to Lily.
He was her very own kangaroo.
Sometimes, Lily would say, "Do you
remember when I first met you?"
And Blue Kangaroo would smile while
Lily told him the whole story all over again.

It seemed like ages and ages ago. Lily had been waiting
for the day when her new baby brother, Jack, would come
home for the first time.

"They're here! They're here!" she cried.
She was so looking forward to helping with everything!

She began straight away!
"Here you are, Mum," she said as she took her
some juice and cookies.
"Thank you, Lily," said her mother. "Be careful
with that tray!"

"Oh! Lily! Look out!"
But it was too late! The vase tipped over…
water and flowers splashed all over Jack's cradle.
"Oh, Lily!" sighed her mother.

Jack screamed and screamed.
"It's all right, Lily," said her mother. "It was an accident."
"Sorry, Jack," said Lily.

When Lily's dad was looking after Jack, Lily said,
"He really can't do anything by himself, can he?"
"That's why he needs you, Lily," said her father.
"Why don't you read to him?"

Lily showed Jack the pictures in her book.
"Here's a cow," she said. "It goes 'mooo!'
And here's a sheep. It goes 'baaa!'
And here's a tiger…" she said,

"…it goes 'RRRRRROOOOOAAAARRRR!'"
Jack shrieked! He screamed and screamed!
"Oh, Lily!" said her father. "That's much too loud!"
"Sorry, Jack," said Lily.

One day, Jack was in his pram in the garden.
"Hello, Jack!" said Lily.

"Shall I rock you and sing a lullaby?
Rock-a-bye baby on the tree top…" she sang.

"When the wind blows, the cradle will rock…"
Lily's singing grew louder and louder.
The pram bounced up and down…
Jack began to cry.

Then he
screamed
and screamed.

"Oh, Lily!"
cried her mother.
"That's much too rough!"
"Sorry, Jack," said Lily.

"I don't think Jack loves me, because he cries whenever
I go near him," said Lily.
"Of course he loves you!" said her father. "You just need
to be gentle with him."

The next day, Lily's grandma came.
"I've got a surprise for you, Lily!" she said.
"I've brought someone who needs looking after!"

Lily's surprise had soft blue ears,
little black eyes, whiskers and a
long blue tail. It was a blue kangaroo!
"Oh!" cried Lily. "I LOVE him!"

Everyone said hello to
Blue Kangaroo.
"I'm going to look after him
for ever and ever!" said Lily.

And Blue Kangaroo
knew he'd come
to the right person.

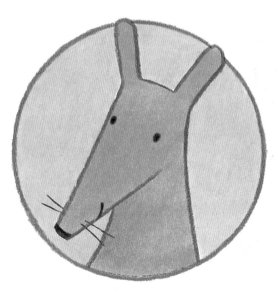

At bedtime, after Jack's bath,
Lily said it was time to bath
Blue Kangaroo.
"You'll love it!" she said, as she
gently put him in the water.

But Blue Kangaroo
wasn't so sure.

"Oh, Blue Kangaroo!" said Lily. "I do love looking after you!"
She sprinkled him with Jack's talcum powder... but it
came out faster than she expected.

It stuck to the wet kangaroo
like glue!
"OH, NO!" cried Lily.
"What's happened to you?"

"Oh dear!
Oh dear!"
thought poor
Blue Kangaroo.

"MUM!" cried Lily.
"Look what I've done!"
"Oh, Lily!" said her mother.

"He'll be all right," said Lily's mother as she gently washed Blue Kangaroo.
"I'm just no good at looking after babies!" said Lily.
"He won't love me now."
"It was just a mistake," said Lily's mother.

"We all make mistakes," she said
as she put Blue Kangaroo in the
airing cupboard to dry.
"You don't!" said Lily.
"That's because I practised on
you!" said Lily's mother.

"Oh…" thought
Blue Kangaroo. "So
Lily needs to practise too."

"Did you make mistakes with me?" asked Lily.
"I make mistakes all the time!" said her mother.
"And I still love you!" said Lily.
"And I love you!" said her mother. "And so do Jack and Blue Kangaroo!"

Lily lay in the dark thinking about her new baby brother
and her new Blue Kangaroo. Everything was new. She
had never looked after anyone smaller than she was.
There were so many new things to learn.

Meanwhile, Blue Kangaroo was feeling better, but he was missing Lily.
"I'd better go and give her a chance to practise looking after me!" he thought.

He jumped a beautiful kangaroo jump,

and landed softly on the floor.

Then he tiptoed
along the passage
to Lily's room.

"Blue Kangaroo!" whispered Lily. "How did you get here?
I didn't know you could do that!"

Blue Kangaroo hopped across the floor and up on to the bed, into Lily's arms.

"Oh, Blue Kangaroo, how clever of you! Will you
help me look after baby Jack too?" said Lily.
She hugged him tight and Blue Kangaroo smiled
his secret smile.
"I knew I'd love you," said Lily, "when I first met you!"
"And I knew I'd love you!" thought Blue Kangaroo.